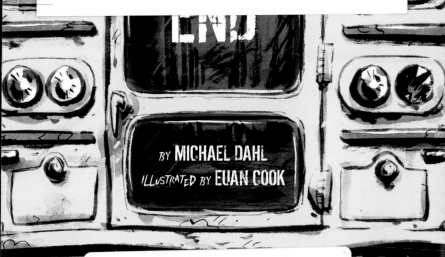

BY MICHAEL DAHL

ILLUSTRATED BY EUAN COOK

Raintree is an imprint of Capstone Global Library Limited, a company incorporated
in England and Wales having its registered office at 264 Banbury Road, Oxford, OX2
7DY – Registered company number: 6695582

www.raintree.co.uk
myorders@raintree.co.uk

Designed by Bob Lentz
Original illustrations © Capstone Global Library Limited 2019
Design element: Cover background by Shutterstock/oldmonk
Production by Tori Abraham
Originated by Capstone Global Library Ltd
Printed and bound in India

ISBN 978 1 4747 5931 1
22 21 20 19 18
10 9 8 7 6 5 4 3 2 1

British Library Cataloguing in Publication Data
A full catalogue record for this book is available from the British Library.

CONTENTS

From dawn to dusk, the **SCHOOL BUS OF HORRORS** rumbles along city streets and down country roads, searching for another passenger. Yellow, black markings, dirty windows – it looks like any other school bus.

But **BEWARE!** Step aboard this bus and

experience the scariest ride of your life . . .

CHAPTER ONE
DEAD MEAT

Braden sits on the bus after school one day.

He stares at a maths test in his hand.

Braden does not want to go home.

At the top of the piece of paper is a large F.

When Mum and Dad find out I failed, Braden thinks, *I am dead meat!*

Braden glances around the bus.

It looks different from the bus that he usually takes home.

The windows are dirty. The floor is covered in mud.

The driver can't be seen. He sits behind a safety wall of thick plastic.

Braden is the last passenger.

The street corner by his house is always the final stop.

"I can't ~~show~~ this test to my parents," he whispers to himself. "Maybe I'll run away."

Then Braden sniffs.

Smells like rotten meat in here, he thinks.

Braden is surprised to feel the bus slowing down.

He leans over to the window.

He wipes away some of the grime with his hand.

The sun has already set.

It is hard to see through the smudged glass.

But Braden sees shadows moving towards the bus.

The road is filled with an endless crowd of people.

CHAPTER TWO
NO ONE SPEAKS

Hundreds and hundreds of people stream past the bus.

Why are they all moving in the same direction? Braden wonders.

The driver stops the bus.

Suddenly, with a whoosh of air,
the door opens.

Braden gets up and walks to the front of the bus.

He stares at the open door.

Then he turns to look back at the plastic wall around the driver.

"Did you open the door?" asks Braden.

The driver does not answer.

Braden slowly walks down the
steps and onto the road.

"What's going on?" he asks
the crowd.

No one speaks.

Braden looks down at the road.

And why isn't anyone wearing shoes?
he wonders.

Braden follows the crowd across the road and down a small slope.

Up ahead is a large wall with a gate.

Above the gate hangs a sign made of curving metal bars: CENTRAL CEMETERY.

CHAPTER THREE
THE GRAVE

A crush of people surround Braden.

He tries to get away, but there are too many bodies.

He yells and shouts, but no one
pays any attention to him.

The crowd pushes and bumps him along.

Suddenly, the crowd stops moving.

He steps forward into a small clearing.

The silent strangers are standing next to a newly dug grave.

It smells like rotting meat.

Braden steps closer to the open grave.

He looks carefully at the stone above the hole.

The dead person's name is in shadow. But Braden can read a date on the stone.

The date is *his* birthday!

Braden feels a sudden chill.

He tries to step away from the grave.

The crowd is closing in on him. Their hands reach out to him.

Braden shouts!

He falls into the open grave.

CHAPTER FOUR
THE LAST STOP

SQUUUUUUEEEEEEEK!

Braden blinks his eyes.

He is sitting on the school bus once more.

The bus stops with a squeal
of brakes.

The door opens.

Braden rushes to the front of the bus.

He peers out of the door and sees a dark street corner.

It is his stop. The last stop.

He sees his house sitting back from the street.

Braden leaps out of the bus.

As soon as his feet hit the pavement, he takes a deep breath.

The test paper is crumpled in his hand.

He doesn't care about the F anymore.

He cannot wait to get home.

GLOSSARY

cemetery place where dead people are buried

glance look at something very quickly

grime dirt or soot that has built up on a surface

passenger someone other than the driver who travels in a vehicle

rotten something that has gone off or started to smell

smudged messy or dirty

DISCUSS

1. Why do you think this book is called *Dead End*?

2. At the beginning of the story, Braden is afraid to go home. At the end, he is happy to finally be at his house. Why do you think his mood changed?

3. What lesson do you think Braden learned from travelling on the School Bus of Horrors?

WRITE

1. Create a new title for this book. Then write a paragraph about why you chose your new title.

2. Write another ending for this book. Maybe Braden doesn't make it home. Maybe he must jump off the moving bus! You decide.

3. Write about the scariest bus journey you've ever experienced.

AUTHOR

MICHAEL DAHL is the author of the Library of Doom series, the Dragonblood books and Michael Dahl's Really Scary Stories. (He wants everyone to know that last title was not his idea.) He was born a few minutes after midnight of April Fool's Day in a thunderstorm, has survived various tornados and hurricanes, as well as an attack from a rampant bunny at night ("It reared up at me!"). He currently lives in a haunted house and once saw a ghost in his high school. He will never travel on a school bus. These stories will explain why.

ILLUSTRATOR

EUAN COOK is an illustrator from London, who enjoys drawing pictures for books and watching foxes and jays out of his window. He also likes walking around looking at broken brickwork, sooty statues and the weird drainpipes and stuff you can find behind old run-down buildings.

SCHOOL BUS OF HORRORS

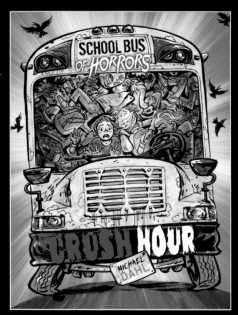